THE MARVELOUS LAND OF OZ

VOL. 3

ADAPTED FROM THE NOVEL BY L. FRANK BAUM

Writer: ERIC SHANOWER
Artist: SKOTTIE YOUNG
Colorist: JEAN-FRANCOIS BEAULIEU
Letterer: JEFF ECKLEBERRY

Assistant Editor: MICHAEL HORWITZ
Editor: NATE COSBY

Collection Editor: MARK D. BEAZLEY
Assistant Editors: ALEX STARBUCK & NELSON RIBEIRO
Editor, Special Projects: JENNIFER GRÜNWALD
Senior Editor, Special Projects: JEFF YOUNGQUIST
SVP of Print & Digital Publishing Sales: DAVID GABRIEL
Production: JERRY KALINOWSKI
Book Design: ARLENE SO

Editor in Chief: AXEL ALONSO
Chief Creative Officer: JOE QUESADA
Publisher: DAN BUCKLEY
Executive Producer: ALAN FINE

Spotlight

MARVEL

visit us at www.abdopublishing.com

Reinforced library bound edition published in 2014 by Spotlight, a division of
the ABDO Group, PO Box 398166, Minneapolis, Minnesota 55439. Spotlight
produces high-quality reinforced library bound editions for schools and libraries.
Published by agreement with Marvel Characters, Inc.

Printed in the United States of America, North Mankato, Minnesota.
102013
012014
This book contains at least 10% recycled materials.

Library of Congress Cataloging-in-Publication Data

Shanower, Eric.
  The marvelous land of Oz / adapted from the novel by L. Frank Baum ; writer:
Eric Shanower ; artist: Skottie Young. -- Reinforced library bound edition.
     pages cm
  "Marvel."
  Summary: When the Scarecrow, now the ruler of the Emerald City, is driven
out by General Jinjur and her all-girl army, his friends--the Tin Woodman, a boy
named Tip, and Jack Pumpkinhead--try to restore peace in this graphic novel ad-
aptation of L. Frank Baum's classic tale.
  ISBN 978-1-61479-235-2 (vol. 1) -- ISBN 978-1-61479-236-9 (vol. 2) -- ISBN
978-1-61479-237-6 (vol. 3) -- ISBN 978-1-61479-238-3 (vol. 4) -- ISBN 978-1-
61479-239-0 (vol. 5) -- ISBN 978-1-61479-240-6 (vol. 6) -- ISBN 978-1-61479-
241-3 (vol. 7) -- ISBN 978-1-61479-242-0 (vol. 8)
  1. Graphic novels. [1. Graphic novels. 2. Fantasy.] I. Young, Skottie, illustrator.
II. Baum, L. Frank (Lyman Frank), 1856-1919. Marvelous land of Oz. III. Title.
  PZ7.7.S453Mar 2014
  741.5'973--dc23
                          2013030127

All Spotlight books are reinforced library binding
and manufactured in the United States of America.

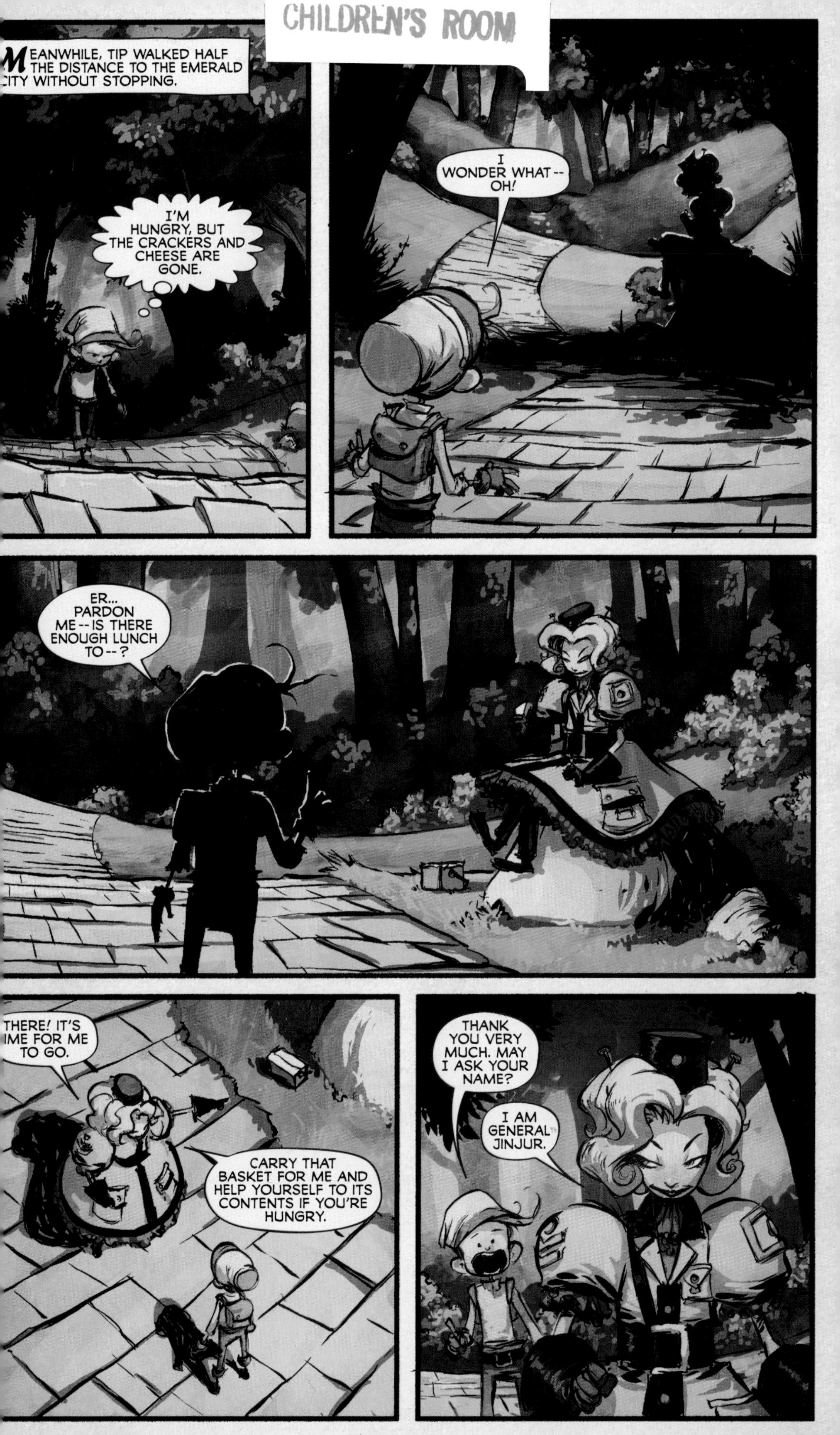
MEANWHILE, TIP WALKED HALF THE DISTANCE TO THE EMERALD CITY WITHOUT STOPPING.
I'M HUNGRY, BUT THE CRACKERS AND CHEESE ARE GONE.
I WONDER WHAT -- OH!
ER... PARDON ME -- IS THERE ENOUGH LUNCH TO --?
THERE! IT'S IME FOR ME TO GO.
CARRY THAT BASKET FOR ME AND HELP YOURSELF TO ITS CONTENTS IF YOU'RE HUNGRY.
THANK YOU VERY MUCH. MAY I ASK YOUR NAME?
I AM GENERAL JINJUR.

WHAT SORT OF A GENERAL?

I COMMAND THE ARMY OF REVOLT IN THIS WAR!

OH! I DIDN'T KNOW THERE WAS A WAR.

YOU WERE NOT SUPPOSED TO KNOW IT -- WE HAVE KEPT IT A SECRET.

AND CONSIDERING THAT OUR ARMY IS COMPOSED ENTIRELY OF GIRLS, IT'S REMARKABLE THAT OUR REVOLT IS NOT YET DISCOVERED.

BUT WHERE'S YOUR ARMY?

ABOUT A MILE FROM HERE. THE FORCES HAVE ASSEMBLED FROM ALL PARTS OF THE LAND OF OZ, AT MY EXPRESS COMMAND.

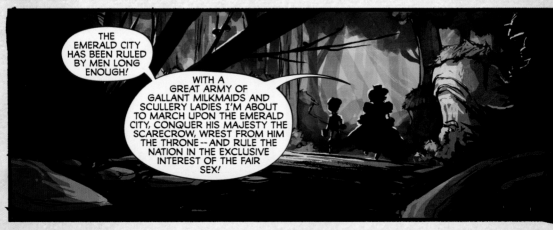

THE EMERALD CITY HAS BEEN RULED BY MEN LONG ENOUGH!

WITH A GREAT ARMY OF GALLANT MILKMAIDS AND SCULLERY LADIES I'M ABOUT TO MARCH UPON THE EMERALD CITY, CONQUER HIS MAJESTY THE SCARECROW, WREST FROM HIM THE THRONE -- AND RULE THE NATION IN THE EXCLUSIVE INTEREST OF THE FAIR SEX!

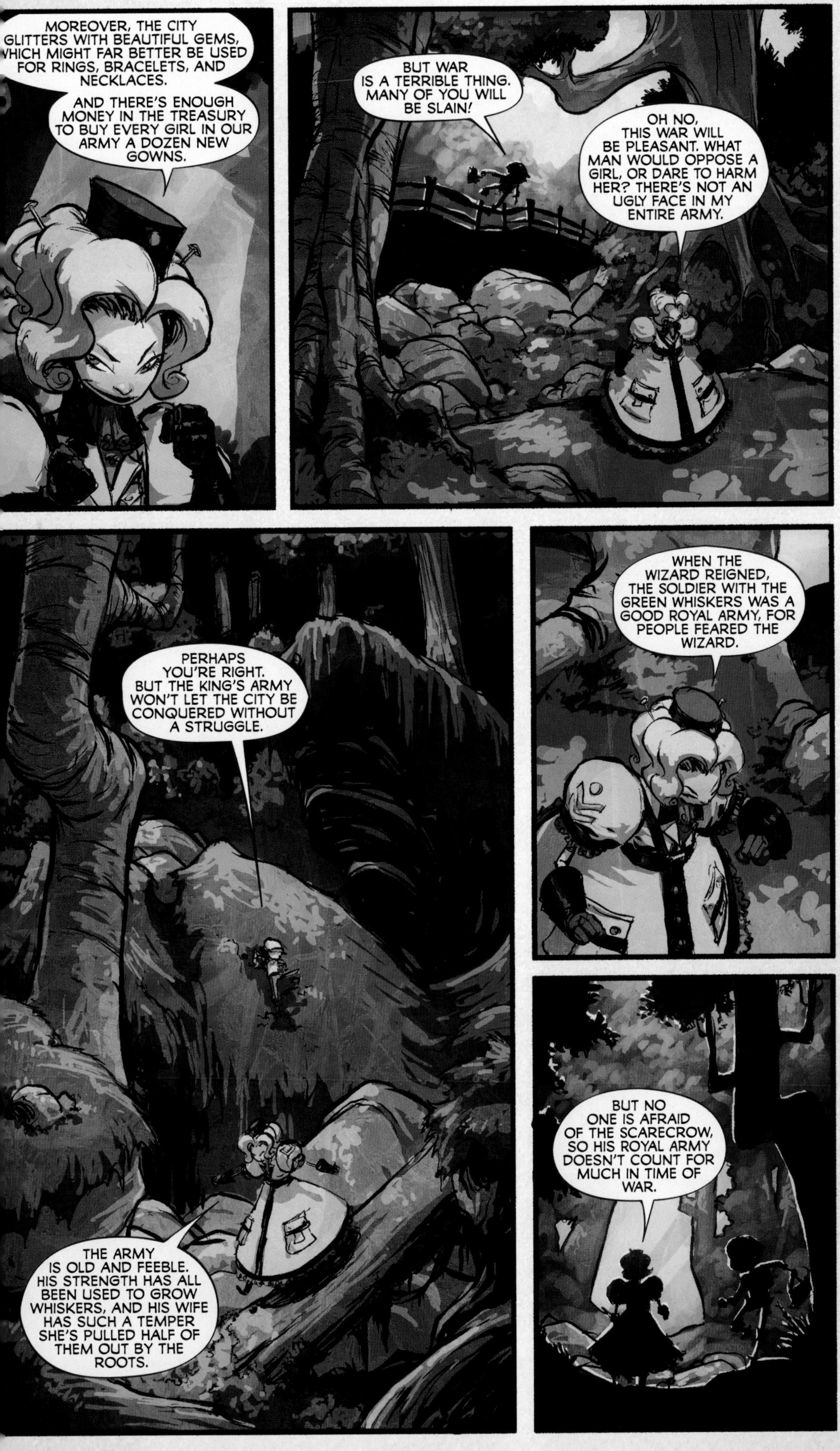
MOREOVER, THE CITY GLITTERS WITH BEAUTIFUL GEMS, WHICH MIGHT FAR BETTER BE USED FOR RINGS, BRACELETS, AND NECKLACES.
AND THERE'S ENOUGH MONEY IN THE TREASURY TO BUY EVERY GIRL IN OUR ARMY A DOZEN NEW GOWNS.
BUT WAR IS A TERRIBLE THING. MANY OF YOU WILL BE SLAIN!
OH NO, THIS WAR WILL BE PLEASANT. WHAT MAN WOULD OPPOSE A GIRL, OR DARE TO HARM HER? THERE'S NOT AN UGLY FACE IN MY ENTIRE ARMY.
PERHAPS YOU'RE RIGHT. BUT THE KING'S ARMY WON'T LET THE CITY BE CONQUERED WITHOUT A STRUGGLE.
THE ARMY IS OLD AND FEEBLE. HIS STRENGTH HAS ALL BEEN USED TO GROW WHISKERS, AND HIS WIFE HAS SUCH A TEMPER SHE'S PULLED HALF OF THEM OUT BY THE ROOTS.
WHEN THE WIZARD REIGNED, THE SOLDIER WITH THE GREEN WHISKERS WAS A GOOD ROYAL ARMY, FOR PEOPLE FEARED THE WIZARD.
BUT NO ONE IS AFRAID OF THE SCARECROW, SO HIS ROYAL ARMY DOESN'T COUNT FOR MUCH IN TIME OF WAR.

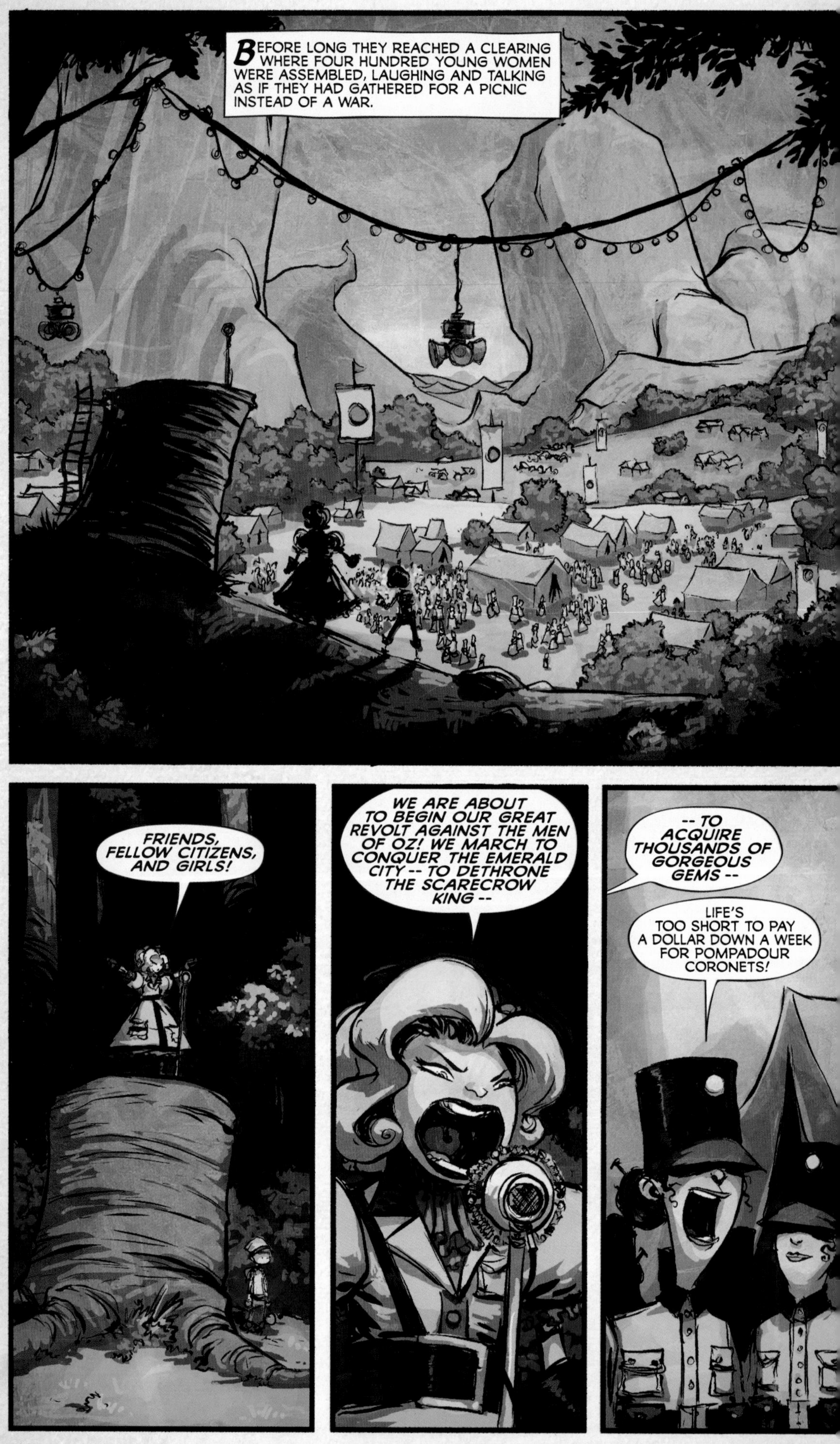
BEFORE LONG THEY REACHED A CLEARING WHERE FOUR HUNDRED YOUNG WOMEN WERE ASSEMBLED, LAUGHING AND TALKING AS IF THEY HAD GATHERED FOR A PICNIC INSTEAD OF A WAR.
FRIENDS, FELLOW CITIZENS, AND GIRLS!
WE ARE ABOUT TO BEGIN OUR GREAT REVOLT AGAINST THE MEN OF OZ! WE MARCH TO CONQUER THE EMERALD CITY -- TO DETHRONE THE SCARECROW KING --
-- TO ACQUIRE THOUSANDS OF GORGEOUS GEMS --
LIFE'S TOO SHORT TO PAY A DOLLAR DOWN A WEEK FOR POMPADOUR CORONETS!

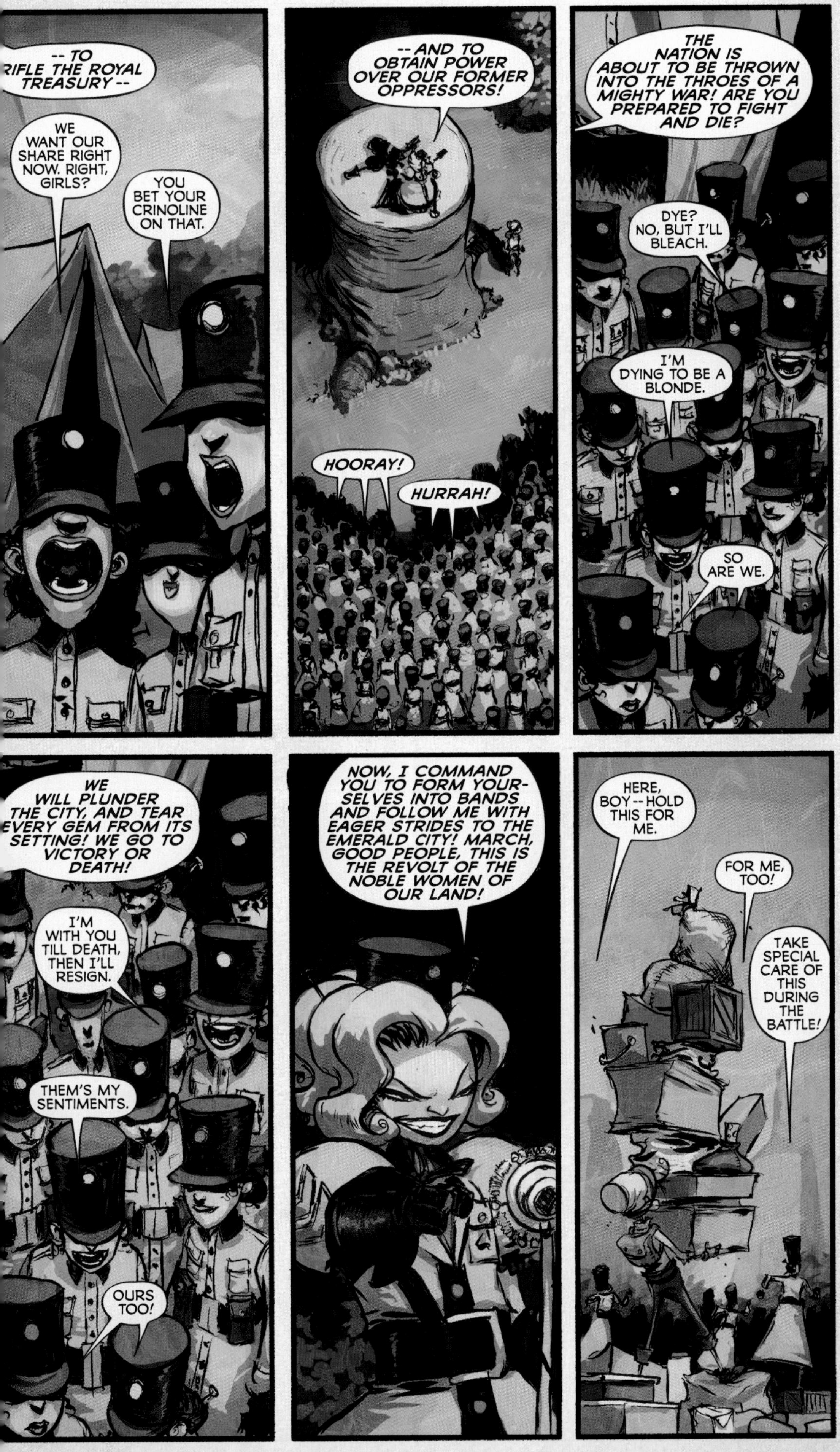
-- TO RIFLE THE ROYAL TREASURY --
WE WANT OUR SHARE RIGHT NOW. RIGHT, GIRLS?
YOU BET YOUR CRINOLINE ON THAT.
-- AND TO OBTAIN POWER OVER OUR FORMER OPPRESSORS!
HOORAY!
HURRAH!
THE NATION IS ABOUT TO BE THROWN INTO THE THROES OF A MIGHTY WAR! ARE YOU PREPARED TO FIGHT AND DIE?
DYE? NO, BUT I'LL BLEACH.
I'M DYING TO BE A BLONDE.
SO ARE WE.
WE WILL PLUNDER THE CITY, AND TEAR EVERY GEM FROM ITS SETTING! WE GO TO VICTORY OR DEATH!
I'M WITH YOU TILL DEATH, THEN I'LL RESIGN.
THEM'S MY SENTIMENTS.
OURS TOO!
NOW, I COMMAND YOU TO FORM YOURSELVES INTO BANDS AND FOLLOW ME WITH EAGER STRIDES TO THE EMERALD CITY! MARCH, GOOD PEOPLE, THIS IS THE REVOLT OF THE NOBLE WOMEN OF OUR LAND!
HERE, BOY -- HOLD THIS FOR ME.
FOR ME, TOO!
TAKE SPECIAL CARE OF THIS DURING THE BATTLE!

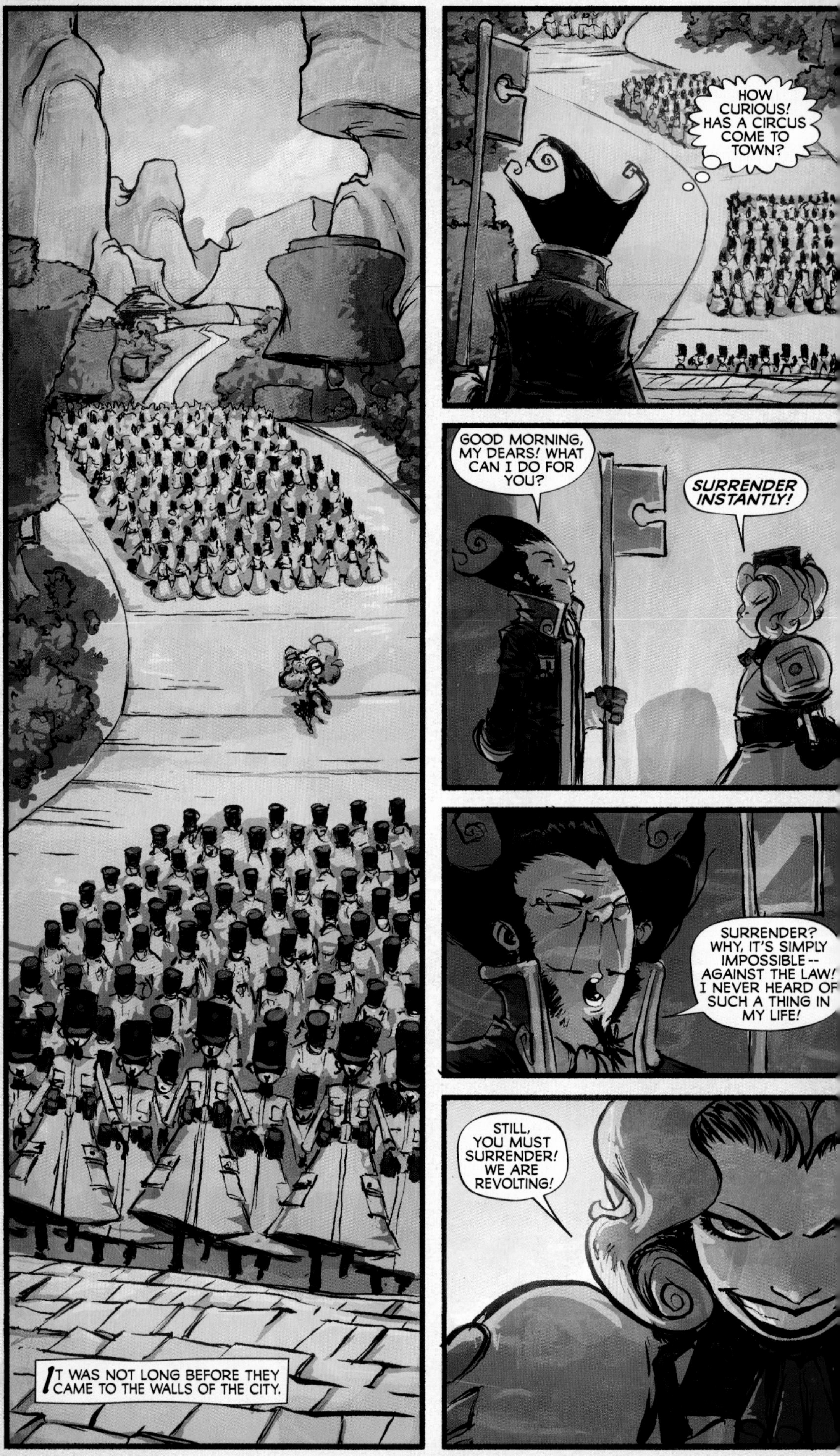
IT WAS NOT LONG BEFORE THEY CAME TO THE WALLS OF THE CITY.
HOW CURIOUS! HAS A CIRCUS COME TO TOWN?
GOOD MORNING, MY DEARS! WHAT CAN I DO FOR YOU?
SURRENDER INSTANTLY!
SURRENDER? WHY, IT'S SIMPLY IMPOSSIBLE-- AGAINST THE LAW! I NEVER HEARD OF SUCH A THING IN MY LIFE!
STILL, YOU MUST SURRENDER! WE ARE REVOLTING!

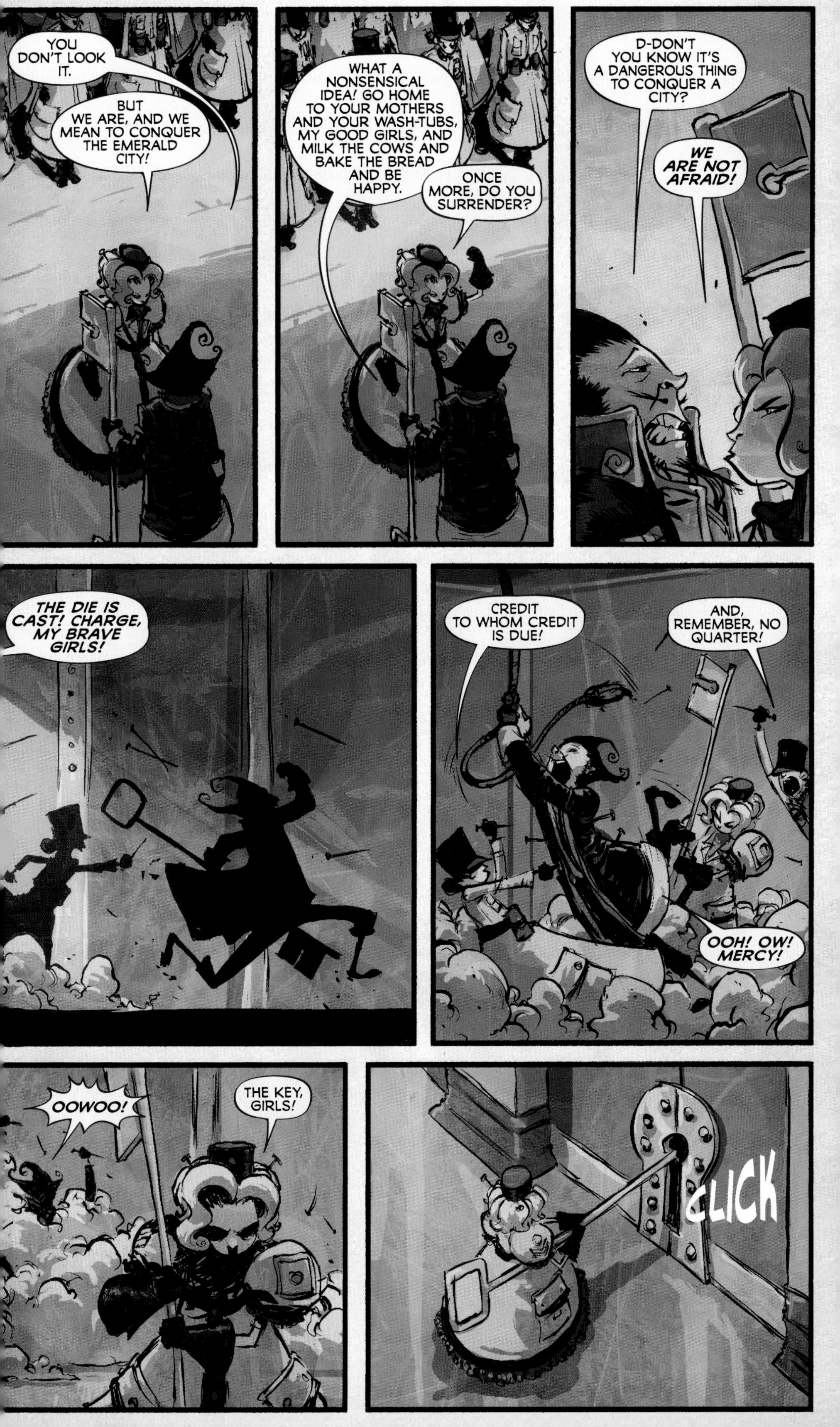
YOU DON'T LOOK IT.
BUT WE ARE, AND WE MEAN TO CONQUER THE EMERALD CITY!
WHAT A NONSENSICAL IDEA! GO HOME TO YOUR MOTHERS AND YOUR WASH-TUBS, MY GOOD GIRLS, AND MILK THE COWS AND BAKE THE BREAD AND BE HAPPY.
ONCE MORE, DO YOU SURRENDER?
D-DON'T YOU KNOW IT'S A DANGEROUS THING TO CONQUER A CITY?
WE ARE NOT AFRAID!
THE DIE IS CAST! CHARGE, MY BRAVE GIRLS!
CREDIT TO WHOM CREDIT IS DUE!
AND, REMEMBER, NO QUARTER!
OOH! OW! MERCY!
OOWOO!
THE KEY, GIRLS!
CLICK

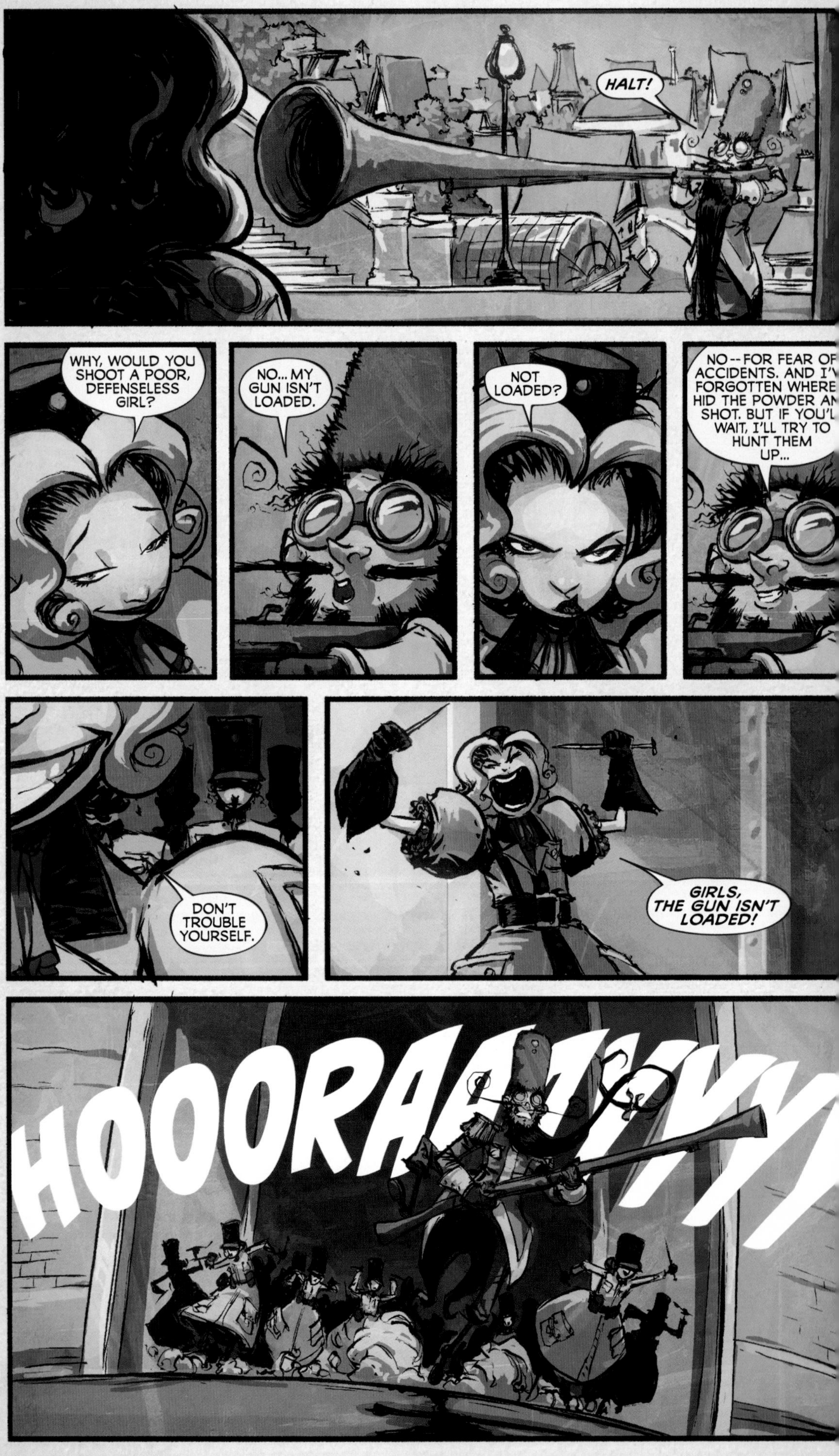
HALT!
WHY, WOULD YOU SHOOT A POOR, DEFENSELESS GIRL?
NO... MY GUN ISN'T LOADED.
NOT LOADED?
NO--FOR FEAR OF ACCIDENTS. AND I'V FORGOTTEN WHERE HID THE POWDER AN SHOT. BUT IF YOU'L WAIT, I'LL TRY TO HUNT THEM UP...
DON'T TROUBLE YOURSELF.
GIRLS, THE GUN ISN'T LOADED!
HOOORAAYYY

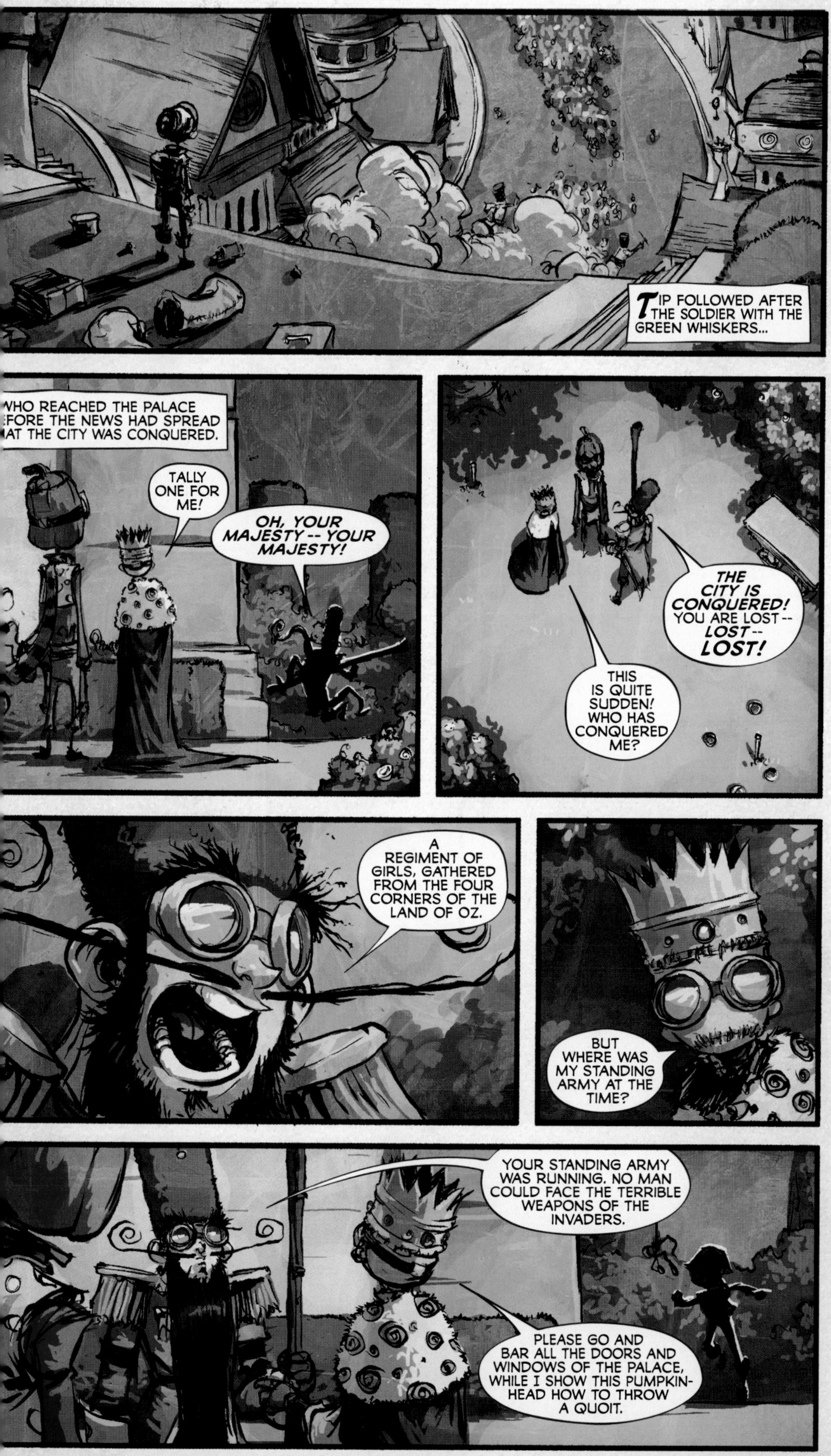
TIP FOLLOWED AFTER THE SOLDIER WITH THE GREEN WHISKERS...
WHO REACHED THE PALACE EFORE THE NEWS HAD SPREAD AT THE CITY WAS CONQUERED.
TALLY ONE FOR ME!
OH, YOUR MAJESTY -- YOUR MAJESTY!
THE CITY IS CONQUERED! YOU ARE LOST -- LOST -- LOST!
THIS IS QUITE SUDDEN! WHO HAS CONQUERED ME?
A REGIMENT OF GIRLS, GATHERED FROM THE FOUR CORNERS OF THE LAND OF OZ.
BUT WHERE WAS MY STANDING ARMY AT THE TIME?
YOUR STANDING ARMY WAS RUNNING. NO MAN COULD FACE THE TERRIBLE WEAPONS OF THE INVADERS.
PLEASE GO AND BAR ALL THE DOORS AND WINDOWS OF THE PALACE, WHILE I SHOW THIS PUMPKIN-HEAD HOW TO THROW A QUOIT.

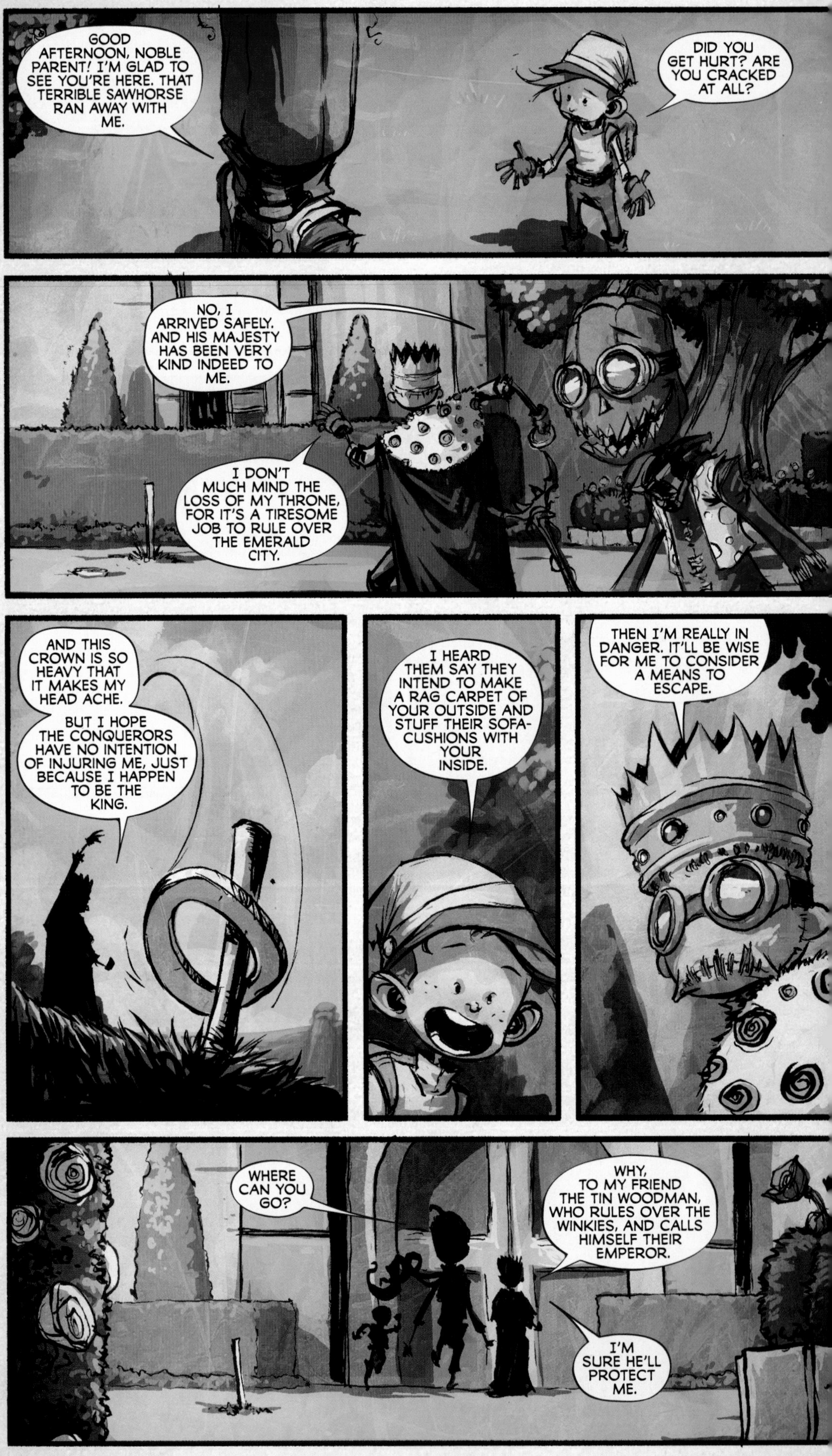
GOOD AFTERNOON, NOBLE PARENT! I'M GLAD TO SEE YOU'RE HERE. THAT TERRIBLE SAWHORSE RAN AWAY WITH ME.
DID YOU GET HURT? ARE YOU CRACKED AT ALL?
NO, I ARRIVED SAFELY. AND HIS MAJESTY HAS BEEN VERY KIND INDEED TO ME.
I DON'T MUCH MIND THE LOSS OF MY THRONE, FOR IT'S A TIRESOME JOB TO RULE OVER THE EMERALD CITY.
AND THIS CROWN IS SO HEAVY THAT IT MAKES MY HEAD ACHE.
BUT I HOPE THE CONQUERORS HAVE NO INTENTION OF INJURING ME, JUST BECAUSE I HAPPEN TO BE THE KING.
I HEARD THEM SAY THEY INTEND TO MAKE A RAG CARPET OF YOUR OUTSIDE AND STUFF THEIR SOFA-CUSHIONS WITH YOUR INSIDE.
THEN I'M REALLY IN DANGER. IT'LL BE WISE FOR ME TO CONSIDER A MEANS TO ESCAPE.
WHERE CAN YOU GO?
WHY, TO MY FRIEND THE TIN WOODMAN, WHO RULES OVER THE WINKIES, AND CALLS HIMSELF THEIR EMPEROR.
I'M SURE HE'LL PROTECT ME.

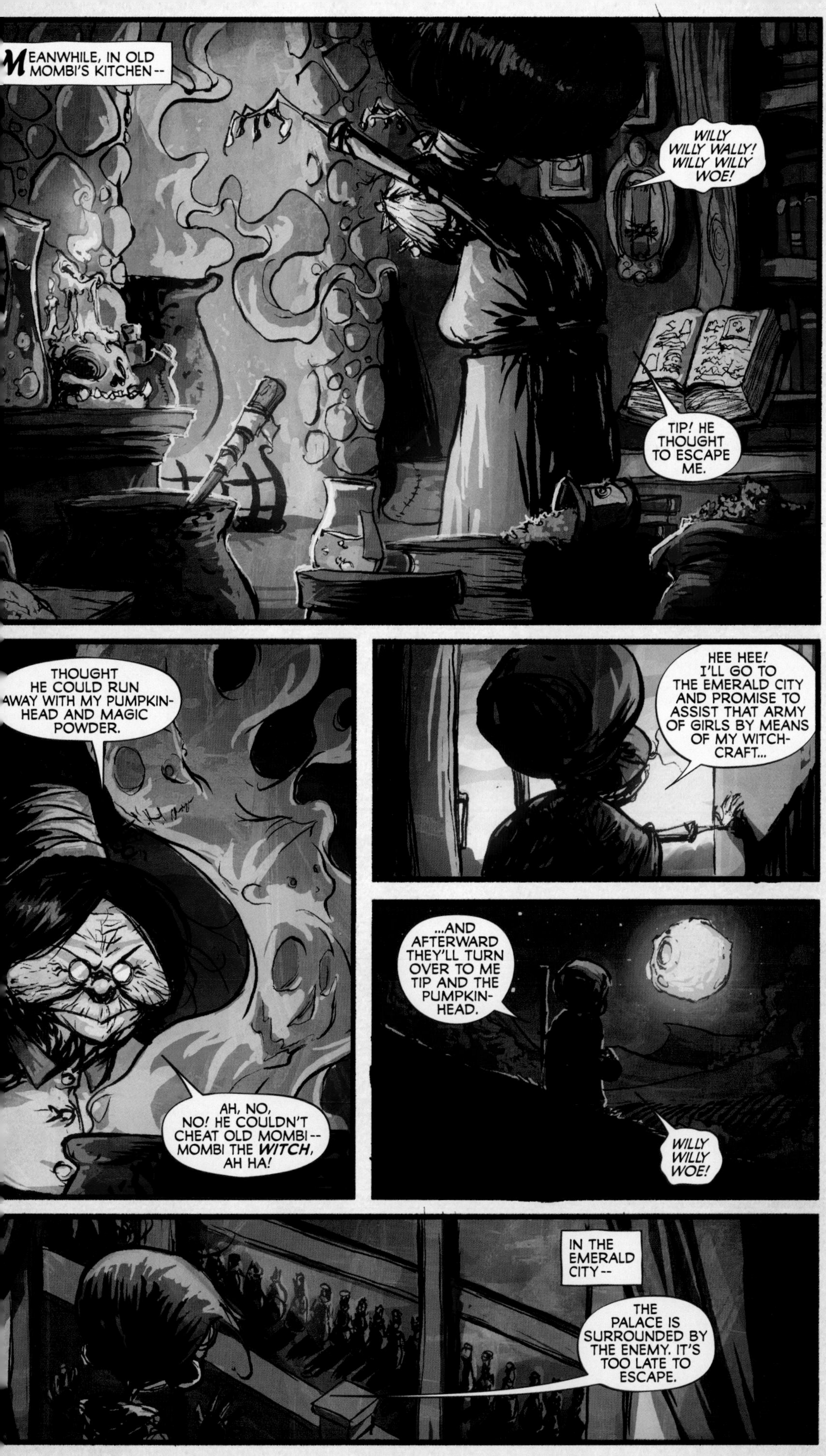
MEANWHILE, IN OLD MOMBI'S KITCHEN--
WILLY WILLY WALLY! WILLY WILLY WOE!
TIP! HE THOUGHT TO ESCAPE ME.
THOUGHT HE COULD RUN AWAY WITH MY PUMPKIN-HEAD AND MAGIC POWDER.
AH, NO, NO! HE COULDN'T CHEAT OLD MOMBI-- MOMBI THE WITCH, AH HA!
HEE HEE! I'LL GO TO THE EMERALD CITY AND PROMISE TO ASSIST THAT ARMY OF GIRLS BY MEANS OF MY WITCH-CRAFT...
...AND AFTERWARD THEY'LL TURN OVER TO ME TIP AND THE PUMPKIN-HEAD.
WILLY WILLY WOE!
IN THE EMERALD CITY--
THE PALACE IS SURROUNDED BY THE ENEMY. IT'S TOO LATE TO ESCAPE.

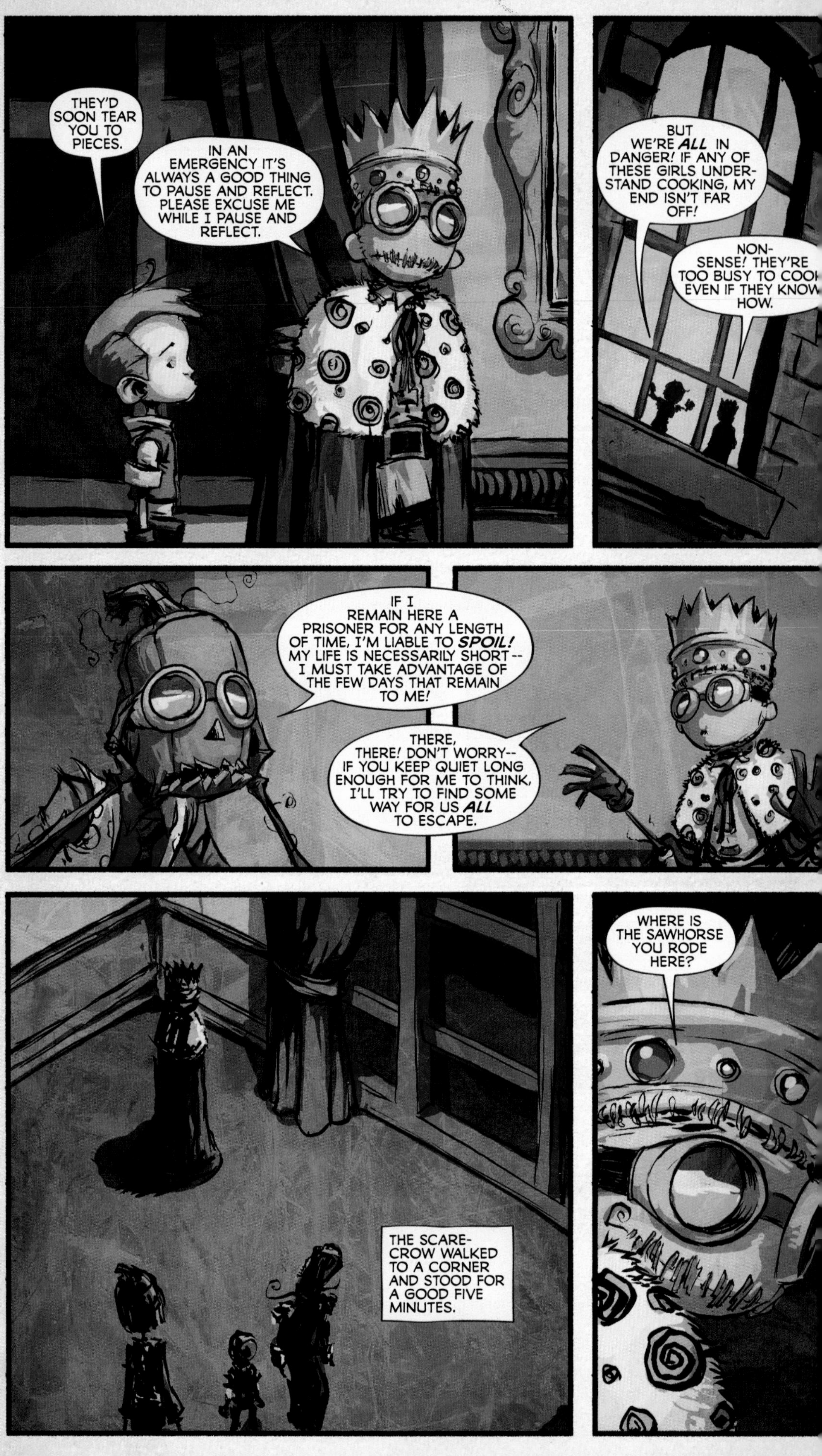
THEY'D SOON TEAR YOU TO PIECES.
IN AN EMERGENCY IT'S ALWAYS A GOOD THING TO PAUSE AND REFLECT. PLEASE EXCUSE ME WHILE I PAUSE AND REFLECT.
BUT WE'RE ALL IN DANGER! IF ANY OF THESE GIRLS UNDERSTAND COOKING, MY END ISN'T FAR OFF!
NONSENSE! THEY'RE TOO BUSY TO COOK EVEN IF THEY KNOW HOW.
IF I REMAIN HERE A PRISONER FOR ANY LENGTH OF TIME, I'M LIABLE TO SPOIL! MY LIFE IS NECESSARILY SHORT-- I MUST TAKE ADVANTAGE OF THE FEW DAYS THAT REMAIN TO ME!
THERE, THERE! DON'T WORRY-- IF YOU KEEP QUIET LONG ENOUGH FOR ME TO THINK, I'LL TRY TO FIND SOME WAY FOR US ALL TO ESCAPE.
THE SCARECROW WALKED TO A CORNER AND STOOD FOR A GOOD FIVE MINUTES.
WHERE IS THE SAWHORSE YOU RODE HERE?

WHY, THE PUMPKINHEAD SAID HE WAS A JEWEL, SO I HAD HIM LOCKED UP IN THE ROYAL TREASURY. IT WAS THE ONLY PLACE I COULD THINK OF, YOUR MAJESTY.

EXCELLENT! BRING THE HORSE HERE AT ONCE.

PRESENTLY--

HE DOESN'T SEEM ESPECIALLY GRACEFUL... BUT I SUPPOSE HE CAN RUN?

HE CAN, INDEED!

THEN, BEARING US UPON HIS BACK, HE MUST DASH THROUGH THE RANKS OF THE REBELS AND CARRY US TO THE TIN WOOD-MAN.

HE CAN'T CARRY FOUR!

NO, BUT HE MAY BE INDUCED TO CARRY THREE. I SHALL THEREFORE LEAVE MY ROYAL ARMY BEHIND.

FOR, FROM THE EASE WITH WHICH HE WAS CONQUERED, I HAVE LITTLE CONFIDENCE IN HIS POWERS.

I EXPECTED THIS BLOW, BUT I CAN BEAR IT.

I SHALL DISGUISE MYSELF BY CUTTING OFF MY LOVELY GREEN WHISKERS.

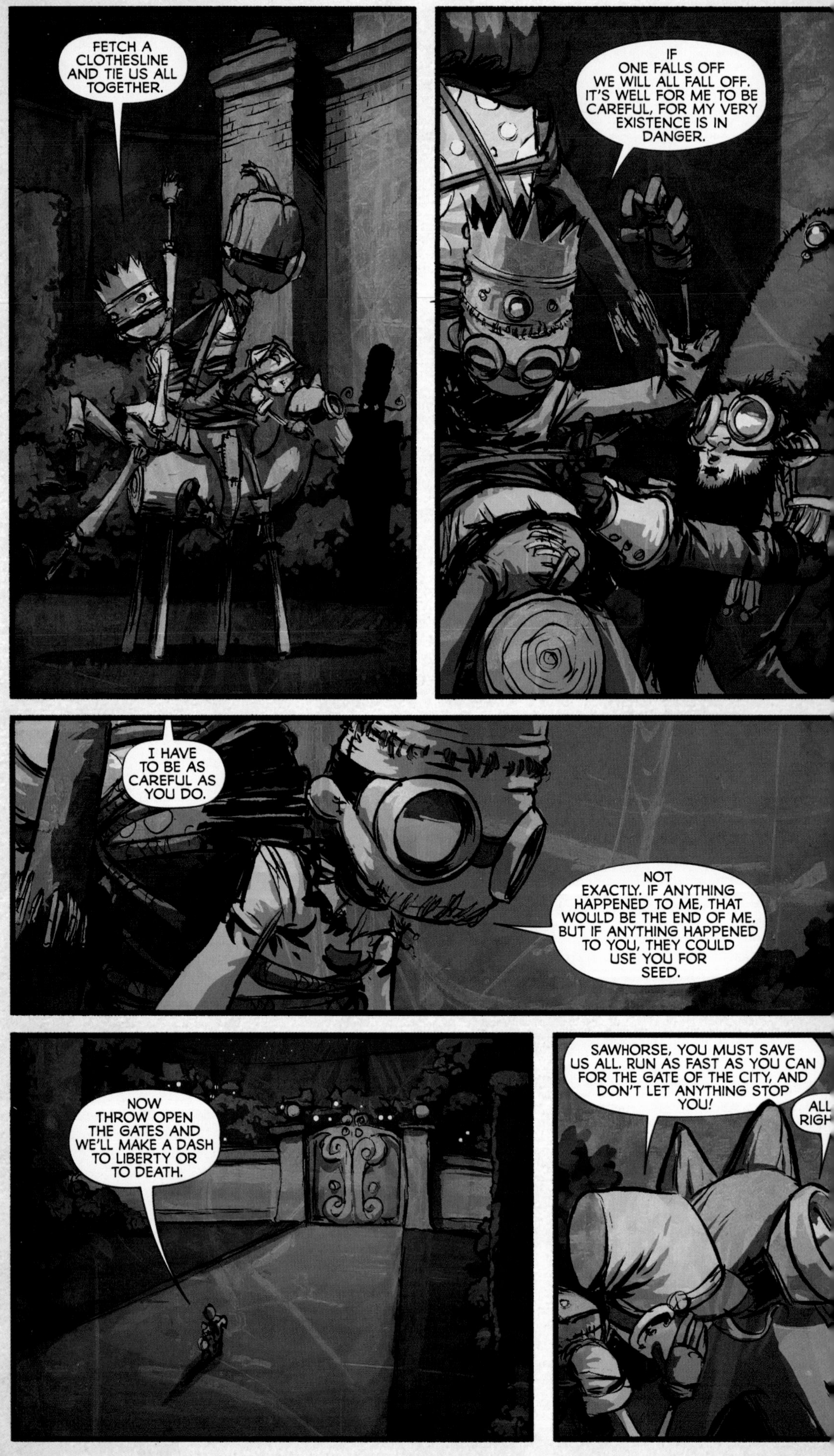

FETCH A CLOTHESLINE AND TIE US ALL TOGETHER.
IF ONE FALLS OFF WE WILL ALL FALL OFF. IT'S WELL FOR ME TO BE CAREFUL, FOR MY VERY EXISTENCE IS IN DANGER.
I HAVE TO BE AS CAREFUL AS YOU DO.
NOT EXACTLY. IF ANYTHING HAPPENED TO ME, THAT WOULD BE THE END OF ME. BUT IF ANYTHING HAPPENED TO YOU, THEY COULD USE YOU FOR SEED.
NOW THROW OPEN THE GATES AND WE'LL MAKE A DASH TO LIBERTY OR TO DEATH.
SAWHORSE, YOU MUST SAVE US ALL. RUN AS FAST AS YOU CAN FOR THE GATE OF THE CITY, AND DON'T LET ANYTHING STOP YOU!

SL-SL-SLOW H-HIM UP-PUP-PUP-PUP! MY STA-STRAW-WAW IS ALL B-BEING SH-SHAKE-SHAKEN--

BUT THE SAW-HORSE'S VIOLENT LEAPS SHOOK THE BREATH OUT OF THE BOY AND HE COULDN'T SPEAK.

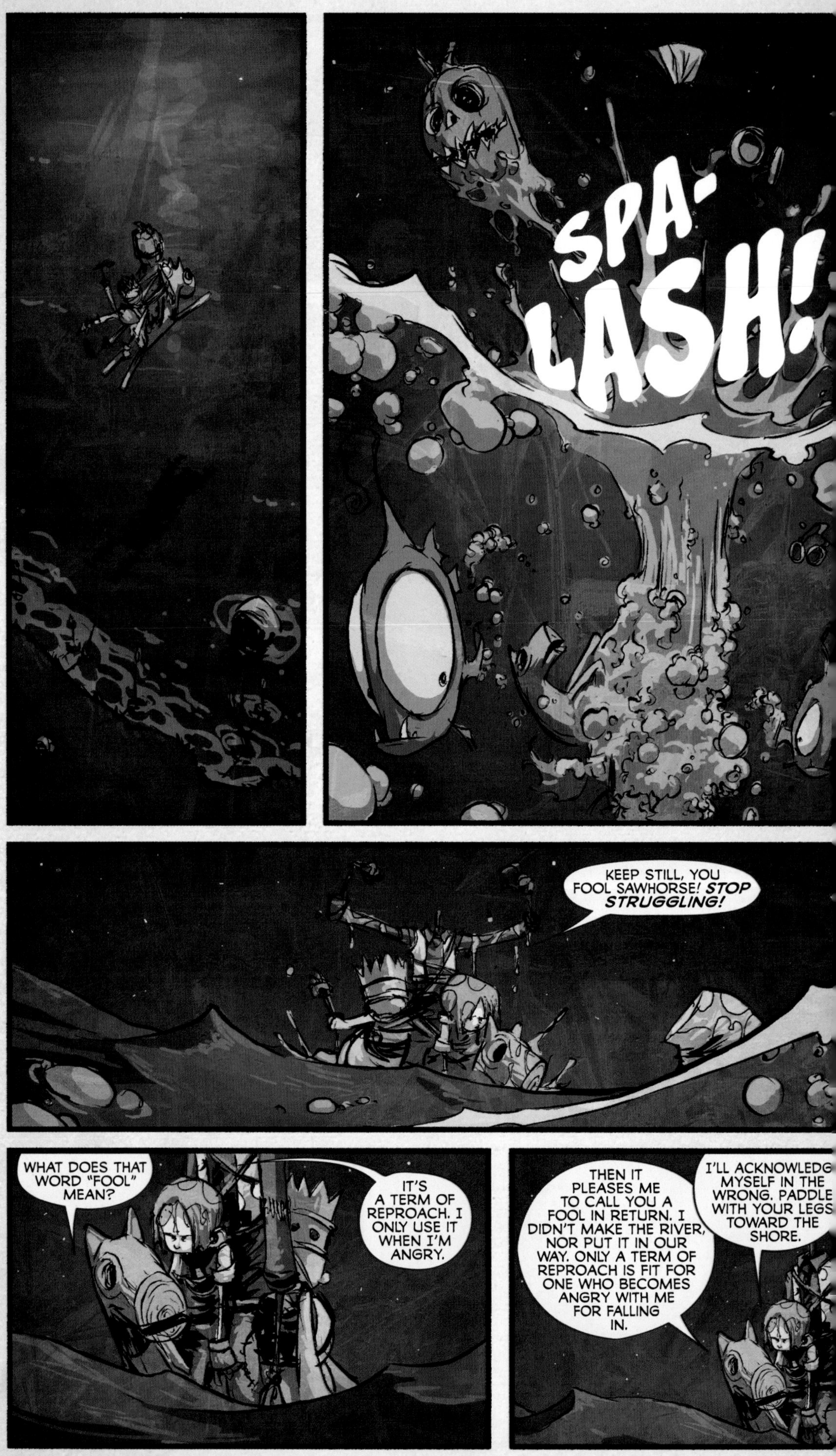
SPA-
LASH!
KEEP STILL, YOU FOOL SAWHORSE! *STOP STRUGGLING!*
WHAT DOES THAT WORD "FOOL" MEAN?
IT'S A TERM OF REPROACH. I ONLY USE IT WHEN I'M ANGRY.
THEN IT PLEASES ME TO CALL YOU A FOOL IN RETURN. I DIDN'T MAKE THE RIVER, NOR PUT IT IN OUR WAY. ONLY A TERM OF REPROACH IS FIT FOR ONE WHO BECOMES ANGRY WITH ME FOR FALLING IN.
I'LL ACKNOWLEDG MYSELF IN THE WRONG. PADDLE WITH YOUR LEGS TOWARD THE SHORE.

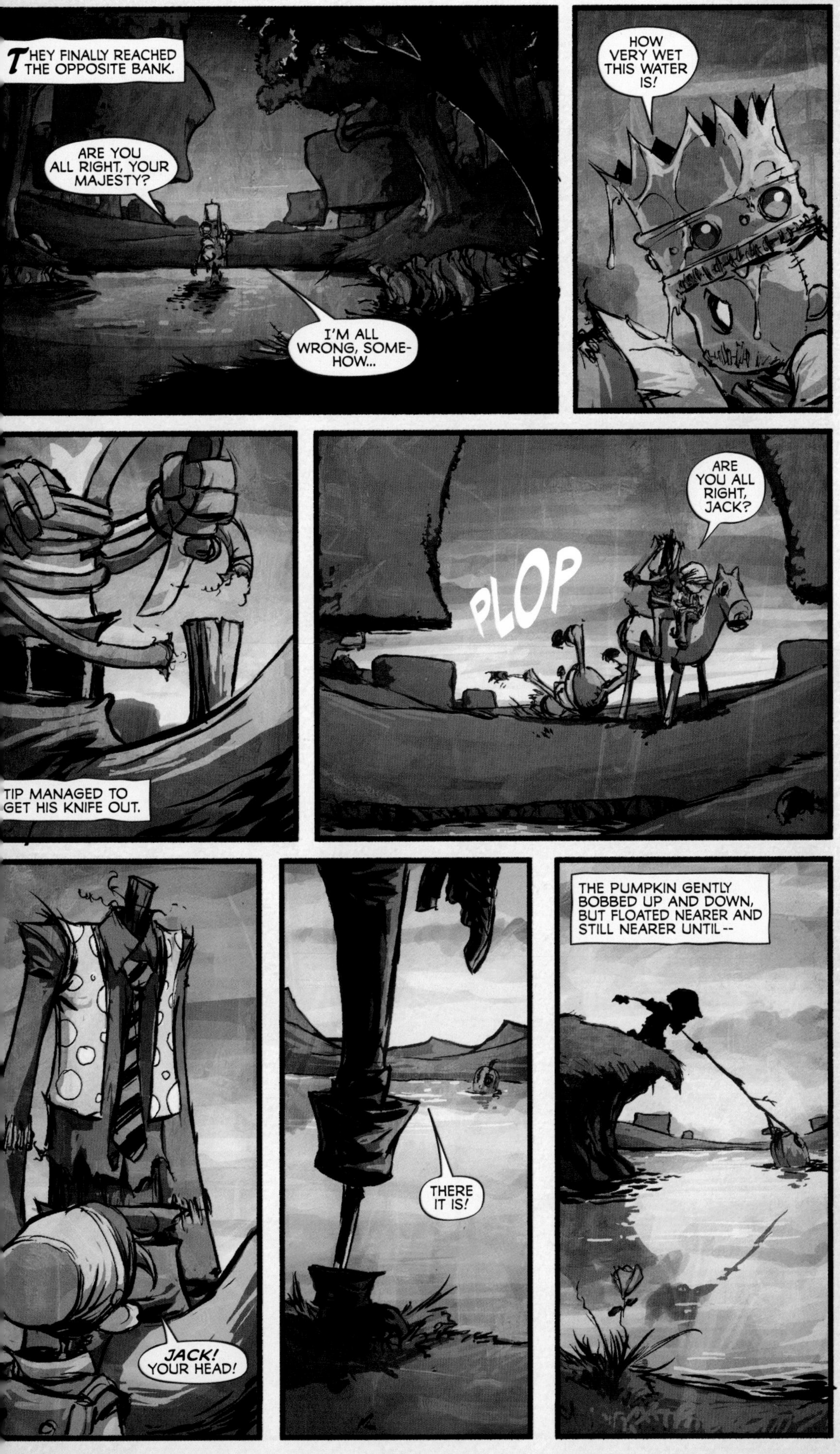
THEY FINALLY REACHED THE OPPOSITE BANK.
ARE YOU ALL RIGHT, YOUR MAJESTY?
I'M ALL WRONG, SOME-HOW...
HOW VERY WET THIS WATER IS!
TIP MANAGED TO GET HIS KNIFE OUT.
PLOP
ARE YOU ALL RIGHT, JACK?
JACK! YOUR HEAD!
THERE IT IS!
THE PUMPKIN GENTLY BOBBED UP AND DOWN, BUT FLOATED NEARER AND STILL NEARER UNTIL--

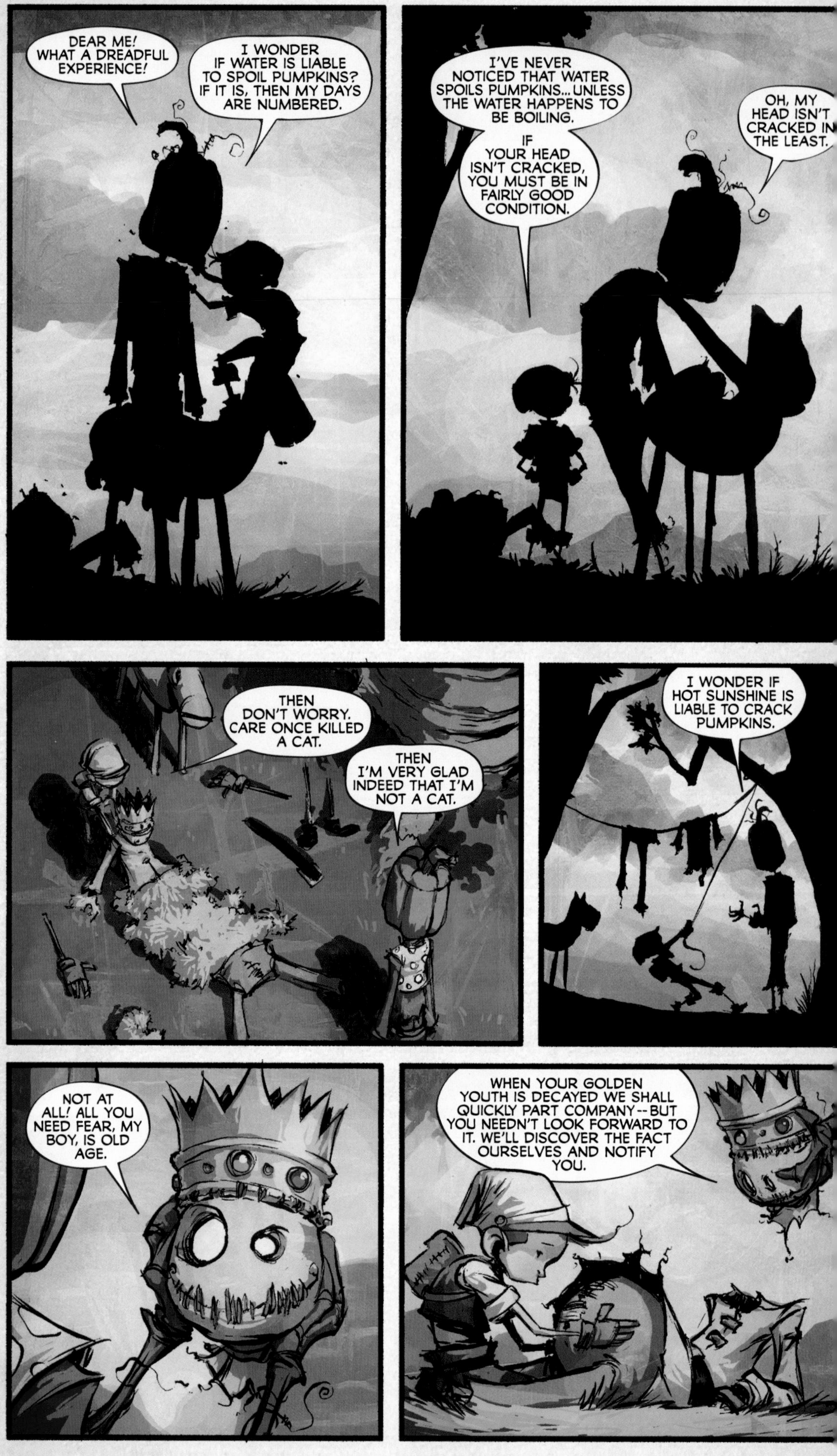
DEAR ME! WHAT A DREADFUL EXPERIENCE!
I WONDER IF WATER IS LIABLE TO SPOIL PUMPKINS? IF IT IS, THEN MY DAYS ARE NUMBERED.
I'VE NEVER NOTICED THAT WATER SPOILS PUMPKINS...UNLESS THE WATER HAPPENS TO BE BOILING.
IF YOUR HEAD ISN'T CRACKED, YOU MUST BE IN FAIRLY GOOD CONDITION.
OH, MY HEAD ISN'T CRACKED IN THE LEAST.
THEN DON'T WORRY. CARE ONCE KILLED A CAT.
THEN I'M VERY GLAD INDEED THAT I'M NOT A CAT.
I WONDER IF HOT SUNSHINE IS LIABLE TO CRACK PUMPKINS.
NOT AT ALL! ALL YOU NEED FEAR, MY BOY, IS OLD AGE.
WHEN YOUR GOLDEN YOUTH IS DECAYED WE SHALL QUICKLY PART COMPANY--BUT YOU NEEDN'T LOOK FORWARD TO IT. WE'LL DISCOVER THE FACT OURSELVES AND NOTIFY YOU.

THANK YOU VERY MUCH. THERE ARE DISTINCT ADVANTAGES IN BEING A SCARE-CROW.

IF ONE HAS FRIENDS NEAR HAND TO REPAIR DAMAGES, NOTHING VERY SERIOUS CAN HAPPEN TO YOU.

BUT COME! LET'S RESUME OUR JOURNEY. I'M ANXIOUS TO GREET MY FRIEND THE TIN WOOD-MAN.

I HOPE THAT HE RULES HIS PEOPLE MORE SUCCESSFULLY THAN I'VE RULED MINE.

GO SLOWLY, SAWHORSE. NOW THERE'S NO DANGER OF PURSUIT.

ALL RIGHT.

AREN'T YOU A LITTLE HOARSE?

SEE HERE, TIP-- CAN'T YOU PROTECT ME FROM INSULT?

I'M SURE JACK MEANT NO HARM.

I'LL HAVE NOTHING MORE TO DO WITH THAT PUMPKINHEAD -- HE LOSES HIS HEAD TOO EASILY.

A FTER A WHILE --

THIS REMINDS ME OF OLD TIMES. IT WAS UPON THIS KNOLL THAT NICK CHOPPER DESTROYED THE GRAY WOLVES OF THE WICKED WITCH OF THE WEST.

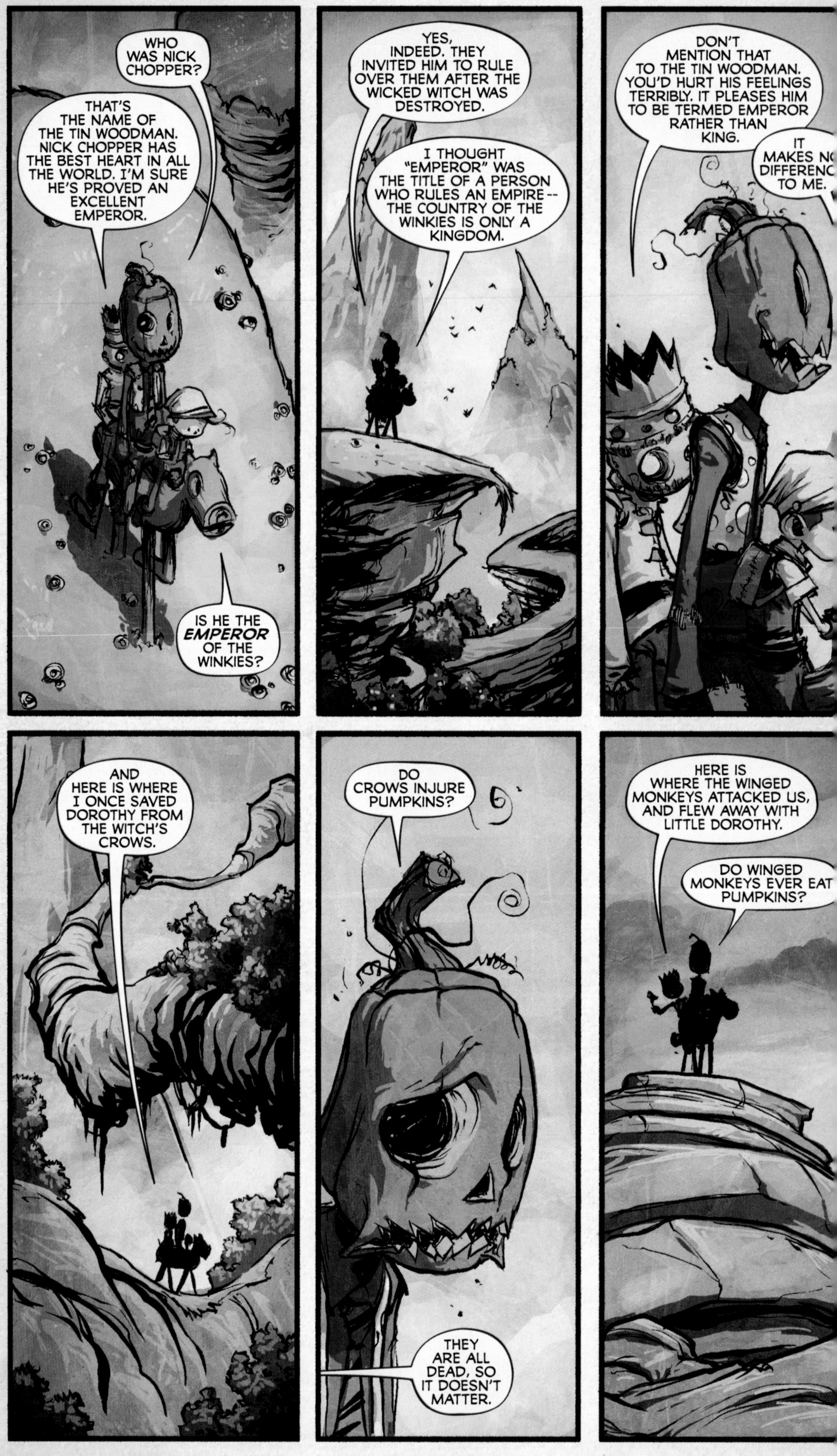
WHO WAS NICK CHOPPER?
THAT'S THE NAME OF THE TIN WOODMAN. NICK CHOPPER HAS THE BEST HEART IN ALL THE WORLD. I'M SURE HE'S PROVED AN EXCELLENT EMPEROR.
IS HE THE *EMPEROR* OF THE WINKIES?
YES, INDEED. THEY INVITED HIM TO RULE OVER THEM AFTER THE WICKED WITCH WAS DESTROYED.
I THOUGHT "EMPEROR" WAS THE TITLE OF A PERSON WHO RULES AN EMPIRE-- THE COUNTRY OF THE WINKIES IS ONLY A KINGDOM.
DON'T MENTION THAT TO THE TIN WOODMAN. YOU'D HURT HIS FEELINGS TERRIBLY. IT PLEASES HIM TO BE TERMED EMPEROR RATHER THAN KING.
IT MAKES NO DIFFERENCE TO ME.
AND HERE IS WHERE I ONCE SAVED DOROTHY FROM THE WITCH'S CROWS.
DO CROWS INJURE PUMPKINS?
THEY ARE ALL DEAD, SO IT DOESN'T MATTER.
HERE IS WHERE THE WINGED MONKEYS ATTACKED US, AND FLEW AWAY WITH LITTLE DOROTHY.
DO WINGED MONKEYS EVER EAT PUMPKINS?

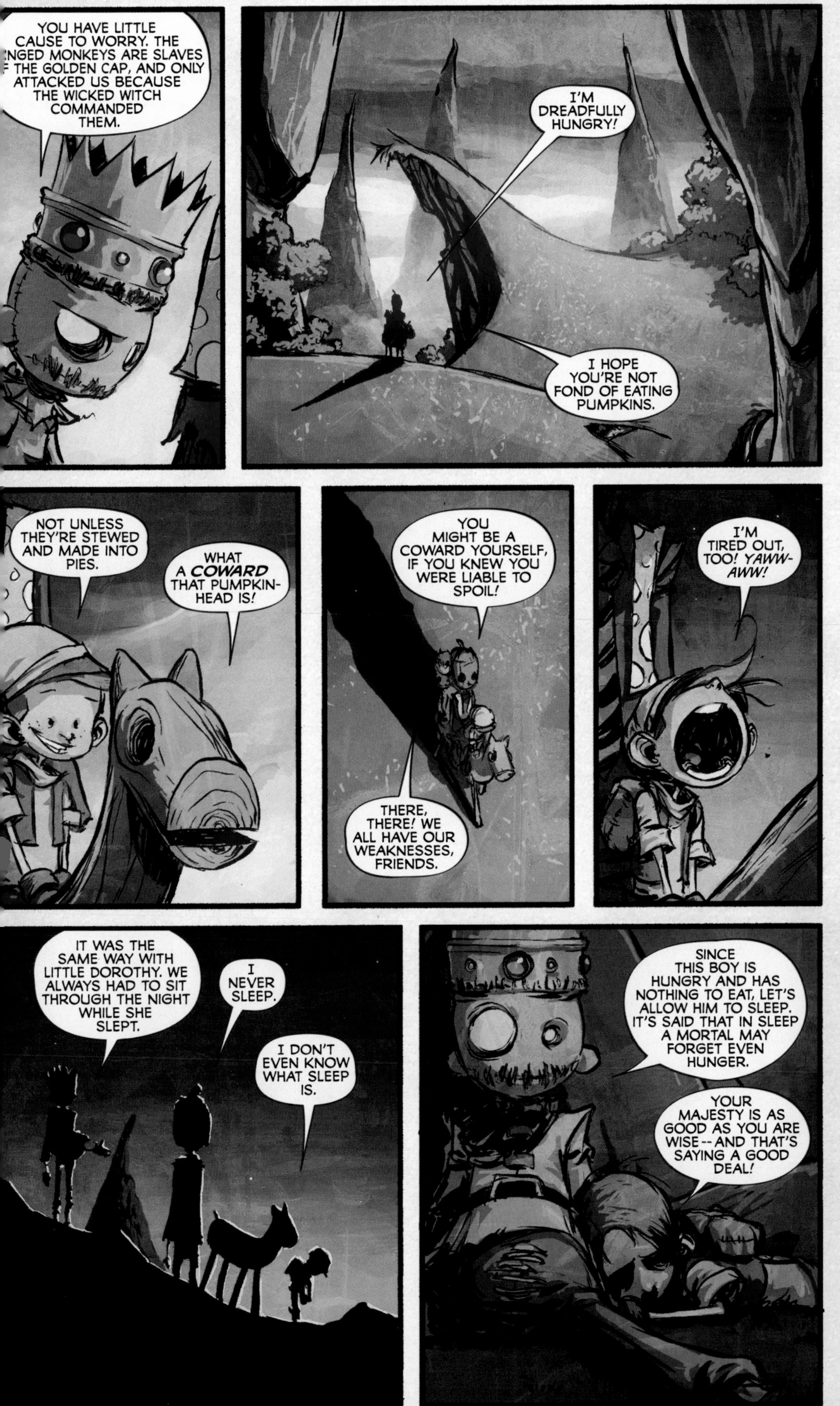
YOU HAVE LITTLE CAUSE TO WORRY. THE NGED MONKEYS ARE SLAVES F THE GOLDEN CAP, AND ONLY ATTACKED US BECAUSE THE WICKED WITCH COMMANDED THEM.
I'M DREADFULLY HUNGRY!
I HOPE YOU'RE NOT FOND OF EATING PUMPKINS.
NOT UNLESS THEY'RE STEWED AND MADE INTO PIES.
WHAT A COWARD THAT PUMPKIN-HEAD IS!
YOU MIGHT BE A COWARD YOURSELF, IF YOU KNEW YOU WERE LIABLE TO SPOIL!
THERE, THERE! WE ALL HAVE OUR WEAKNESSES, FRIENDS.
I'M TIRED OUT, TOO! YAWW-AWW!
IT WAS THE SAME WAY WITH LITTLE DOROTHY. WE ALWAYS HAD TO SIT THROUGH THE NIGHT WHILE SHE SLEPT.
I NEVER SLEEP.
I DON'T EVEN KNOW WHAT SLEEP IS.
SINCE THIS BOY IS HUNGRY AND HAS NOTHING TO EAT, LET'S ALLOW HIM TO SLEEP. IT'S SAID THAT IN SLEEP A MORTAL MAY FORGET EVEN HUNGER.
YOUR MAJESTY IS AS GOOD AS YOU ARE WISE--AND THAT'S SAYING A GOOD DEAL!

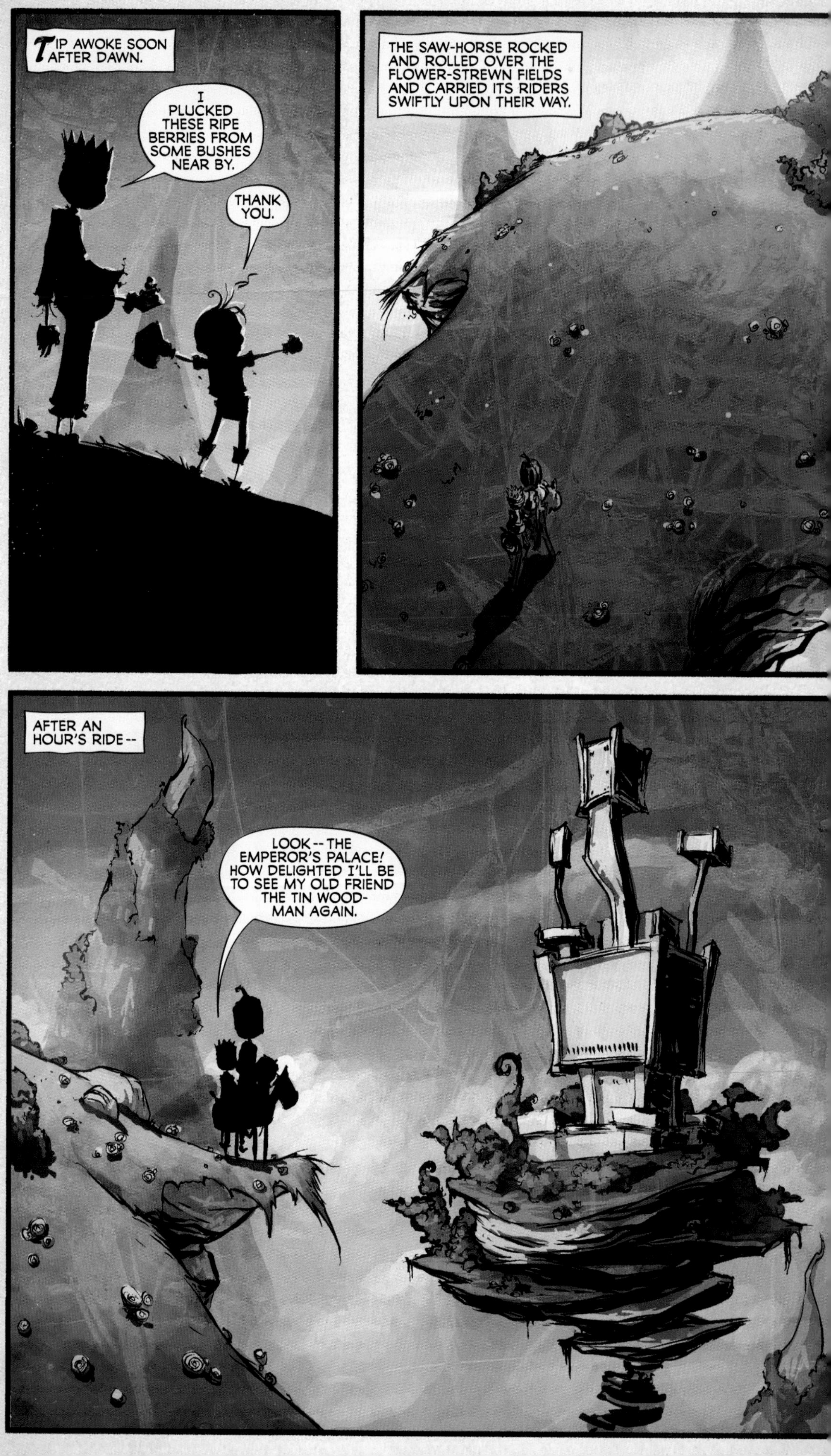
TIP AWOKE SOON AFTER DAWN.
I PLUCKED THESE RIPE BERRIES FROM SOME BUSHES NEAR BY.
THANK YOU.
THE SAW-HORSE ROCKED AND ROLLED OVER THE FLOWER-STREWN FIELDS AND CARRIED ITS RIDERS SWIFTLY UPON THEIR WAY.
AFTER AN HOUR'S RIDE--
LOOK--THE EMPEROR'S PALACE! HOW DELIGHTED I'LL BE TO SEE MY OLD FRIEND THE TIN WOOD-MAN AGAIN.